## THOMAS GRAY'S ELEGY

托马斯·格雷(Thomas Gray,1716—1771)，于伦敦一经纪人家庭。入伊顿公学和剑桥波尔游大陆。1742年起定居剑桥，从事接受。1759至1761年在伦敦新建的不列1768年任剑桥大学历史和近代语教授。物学、昆虫学都感兴趣。他的英国湖区文字优美见称。

英国18世纪新古典主义后期的重要诗人，出生大学。1739年至1741年陪同学霍拉斯·沃创作。1757年被提名为桂冠诗人，但未颠博物馆钻研冰岛及威尔士古代诗歌。格雷除写诗外，学过法律，对考古和植《纪游》(1775)和《书信集》(1775)都以

格雷一生只写过十几首诗。最早的《春短暂，人不论贫富或地位高低都不免一死的思感叹学童未来将经受的不幸。《坎坷》(1742)，同样

天颂》(1742)，描写春天的大自然，表现人生思。《伊顿远眺》(1742)，在描写风景的同时，以不论善恶，等待人们的都是厄运为主题。

格雷最著名的诗是《墓园挽歌》(1750)，全诗128行，用8年时间写成。诗中突出体现了对默默无闻的农民的同情，惋惜他们没有机会施展天赋，批评大人物的傲慢和奢侈。对暮色中大自然的描写，对下层人民的同情,感伤的情调，使这首诗成为浪漫主义诗歌的经典，在艺术技巧上又达到了古典主义诗艺的完美境界。

格雷还以古希腊诗人品达罗斯的颂歌体写了《诗歌的进程》(1759)和《歌手》(1757)。前者追溯诗歌从希腊到英国的发展变化，称颂莎士比亚、弥尔顿、德莱顿；后者写古代威尔士最后一个歌手对13世纪囚吞并威尔士的英王爱德华一世的诅咒。

他还翻译了北欧诗歌《命运女神姐妹》(1761)和《奥丁的降世》(1761)，开浪漫派对北欧文学感兴趣的先风。

文爱艺，当代著名作家、诗人、翻译从小精读古典诗词，十四岁开始发表作

家，中国作家协会会员。生于湖北省襄阳市，品。

著有《春祭》《梦裾》(2版)《夜花》(4版)《雨中花》(2001—2002)坐爱情之外》《梦的岸边》《流逝在花的月亮》《伴月星》《一帘梦》《雪花结队的梦》《我的灵魂是火焰·文爱艺敞开的花朵·文爱艺散文诗选集(1976—《文爱艺诗歌精品赏析集》(全三卷)《文红莲·白雪唤醒的纯洁/赏析版·典藏本》《文爱艺（10版·插图本）《文爱艺诗集》(11版·插图本)《文爱艺全集》(诗1—4卷·数字版)

夜秋雨》(2版)《太阳花》(9版)《寂寞病玫瑰》(2003—2004)《温柔》《独朵里的记忆》《生命的花朵》《长满翅膀的心情》《来不及摇醒的美丽》《成群抒情诗选集(1976—2000)》《像心一样2000)》《文爱艺爱情诗集·玫瑰花园》爱艺抒情诗集(全三册)追逐彩蝶·斯桥边的抒情诗集》《文爱艺散文诗集》《文爱艺爱情诗集》等60多部诗集，深受读者喜爱，再版不断。

部分作品被译成英语、法语、世界语等文，现主要致力于系列小说的创作。

译有《勃朗宁夫人十四行爱情诗集》（插图本）《亚当夏娃日记》（10版·插图本）《柔波集》（插图本）《恶之花》（9版·全译本·赏析版·插图本）《爱的心之》《奢侈品之战》《沉思录》（6版·插图本）《箴言录》（6版·插图本）《思想录》（插图本）《古埃及亡灵书》（2版·灵魂之书·插图本）《小王子》（2版·插图本）《一个孩子的诗园》（8版·插图本）《天真之歌》（插图本）《经验之歌》（插图本）《亚瑟王传奇》（2版·插图本）《墓畔挽歌》（2版·插图本）《老人与海》（3版·插图本）《培根随笔全集》等经典名著及其他著作。

编著有《离骚》《天问》《九歌》《九章》《九辨》《绝句》《花之魂》《中国古代风俗百图》（2版·插图本）《道德经》《金刚经》《心经》《茶经》《酒经》《草书·元·鲜于枢书唐诗》《行书·宋·米芾天马赋》《诗二十四品》《孟浩然全集》《陈子昂全集》《中国时间》《中国病人》《静心录》《净心录》《洗冤集录》》；《经典书库》《新诗金库》《品质书库》《品质诗库》等书。

另出版有《当代寓言大观》（4卷）《当代寓言名家名作》（9卷）《当代寓言金库》（10卷）《开启儿童智慧的100个当代寓言故事》等少儿读物。

所著、译、编图书，连获2015年（首届）、2016年"海峡两岸十大最美图书"奖，连续4届及2015年、2016年、2017年共7届10部"中国最美图书"奖，《文爱艺诗集》获"世界最美图书"奖。

共出版著述200余部。

# THOMAS GRAY'S ELEGY

## ELEGY WRITTEN IN A COUNTRY CHURCH-YARD

*by Thomas Gray: illustrated with wood-engravings,
sketched in that same churchyard at Stoke Poges,
by Agnes Miller Parker;and with an introduction*

# 墓畔挽歌 中文首译全本

[英] 托马斯·格雷 著

文爱艺 译

[英] 艾格尼斯·米勒·帕克 木刻插图

中央编译出版社

# 内容简介

托马斯·格雷（Thomas Gray，1716—1771），是英国18世纪新古典主义后期的重要诗人，"墓畔派"的代表人物；墓畔派诗人是指18世纪描写死亡与哀挽的诗人，《墓畔挽歌》是墓畔派最著名的作品，也是托马斯·格雷的代表作。

本书是《墓畔挽歌》中文首译本，由著名作家、诗人文爱艺先生耗时十余年精心译迻。

格雷出生在伦敦的一个经纪人家庭，一生的大部分时间在剑桥大学从事教学与研究工作。

格雷一生作诗不多，虽只写过几十首诗，仅十余首传世，但他为18世纪的英国，也为世界奉献了一部最著名的诗篇——《墓畔挽歌》(Elegy Written in a Country Church-Yard)。此诗使他成为18世纪最著名的诗人，此诗也是迄今依然存活于人心的诗篇。虽然他不慕功名，谢绝"桂冠诗人"的称号。

《墓畔挽歌》创作长达8年之久，最初是为了哀悼他在伊顿公学读书时的好友里查德·韦斯特，诗末所附的"墓志铭"即为后者而作。格雷以个人的情感和亲身经历，对死亡和生命的奥秘进行了深刻的思考。纵观全诗，内容已明显超越了对某个具体人物的哀思，而是通过对乡村墓地的描写，表达对下层默默无闻的人民的深切同情，对他们纯朴善良品质的赞扬，为他们没有机会施展天赋和才华而惋惜，同时也表现了对权贵、人间虚荣的蔑视和嘲讽，对大人物傲慢奢侈生活的谴责。他把平民百姓和大人物加以比较，分析了在机遇相等的情况下，他们所能做出的成就。他同情穷人和小人物，而嘲讽那些瞧不起穷人、欺负穷人的所谓"大人物"。

诗探讨了死亡和生命这两个沉重的话题。从开篇描绘一幅幅乡野里农民丰收祥和的画面，到对散落的墓志铭的刻写，体现了作者对平凡简单生活的赞扬以及对权贵冷漠的鞭挞。强烈的对比体现出了特定的时代风貌；在命运和机会无法垂青的背景下，普通人即使勤劳勇敢、满腔热血，也无法大展身手，赢得一番作为，最后只得带着遗憾，葬身荒野，留下不忍卒读的墓碑，了此一生。相反，权贵们打着高贵的幌子轻蔑穷苦的平民，讥讽善良和仁慈。如此不对等的社会背景，是诗的创作来源，格雷联系个人的情感和亲身经历，在诗中展露了浓重的哀伤和惋惜。

诗充分体现了民主思想，真切地表达了托马斯·格雷的民主情怀。贫困使农民不能发挥自己的才能，不能成为像弥尔顿那样的文学家、克伦威尔那样的政治家。但是他们身上没有"骄奢""傲慢""野心"和"谄媚"。他们虽然"贫瘠"，没有知识，却有"德性"和"天良"，他们是自然本身。这样的思想和弥漫于全诗的感伤情调，使《墓畔挽歌》成为感伤主义诗歌的典范之作。

《墓畔挽歌》历代注评不断，因为"它凝聚了人类社会中绵延至今的一种情绪，并以完美的形式表达了这种情绪，具有杰出的艺术成就"。

《墓畔挽歌》，从古典主义迈向浪漫主义的国度。诗的语言精雕细琢，抒发了对自然以及人与人之间和谐关系的渴望。深层的感伤、叹惋在精美的诗歌形式中架构起来，有着动人心弦的魅力。

《墓畔挽歌》已经成为百余年来英文世界的必读书。

# 目录

CONTENTS

011 序

033 墓畔挽歌

125 跋

# 序

INTRODUCTION

I

There is something incongruous, I think, in the picture we have of the small, reserved, arrogant, effeminate figure of the little poet sheltering behind the great walls of Pembroke College and the world-wide resounding, undiminishing glories of that poet's most famous poem. Not that the poem does not belong to the poet, but the psychological interest in Thomas Gray is that it is only at rare, suddenly lit moments that we see into the soul of Gray. The year before he died there was this little portrait of him: "Mr. Gray's singular niceness in the choice of his acquaintances makes him appear fastidious in a great degree to all who are not acquainted with his manner. He is of a fastidious and recluse distance of carriage, rather averse to all sociability but of the graver turn, nice and elegant in his person, dress and behaviour, even to a degree of finicality and effeminacy."

我想，我们都不难发现，诗人的画中形象与文学盛名间有种不协调：画中，彭布罗克学院的高墙后庇护着的可怜诗人，看起来矮小，保守，高傲而又柔弱；现实中，他最负盛名的诗歌享有世界声誉，广为传颂，经久不衰。我不是说此诗并非出自这位诗人之手，而是说很少能有这么一首代表着托马斯·格雷真正内心志趣的诗，瞬间点燃我们审视托马斯·格雷灵魂的欲念。在他逝世的前一年，有这样一小段描述他的话：

"格雷先生对于择友格外讲究，这很大程度上使得那些不了解他行为方式的人认为他是一个挑剔的人。他为人挑剔、孤僻，而且厌恶所有社交活动，但严格来说，他称得上是一个品性善良、温文尔雅、穿着讲究、举止得体之人，甚至某种程度上，有些做作和阴柔。"

He was, undoubtedly, effeminate in his manner, reserved, often arrogant and rude to those whom he did not know, icy and hard on occasions, and capable of grim sarcasm. So much of the superficial man. The real Gray wrote one of the dozen great poems in the English language and was, for my own taste, the most enchanting letter writer who ever lived, with Madame de Sévigné, Edward Fitzgerald and Byron close behind him; he was one of the most loyal friends and was capable of a real and deep passion in friendship even at the very end of his life when he was an aged and sick man. He was one of the most tender, chivalrous and unselfish of sons and could be, when he trusted his company, one of the merriest talkers in Europe.

毫无疑问，他在举止上略显柔弱、内敛，常常对他并不熟悉的人流露出傲慢、粗鲁的神色。有时候还有些冷淡严酷，极尽挖苦之力，尽显一个肤浅人的行为举止。然而，在为数不多的伟大的英文诗歌中，其中一首正是出自格雷之手，在我看来，他是有史以来最具魅力的书信体作家，引塞维涅夫人（法国书信作家）、爱德华·菲茨杰拉德（英国诗人、翻译家）和拜伦（英国浪漫主义时期杰出诗人）紧随其后。他对朋友最为忠诚，纵使在生命的尽头，年迈羸弱的他依然对友谊抱有深厚真切的热情。他侠骨柔情，无私慷慨，一旦同伴获得了他的信任，他便口若悬河，成为欧洲数一数二的健谈者。

*

The exterior story of his life is very simple. Thomas Gray was born at his father's house in Cornhill, London, on the 26th December, 1716. Oddly enough, of his ancestry practically nothing is known. Late in life, when he was famous, Baron Gray of Gray in Forfarshire claimed a relationship. All Gray said was: "I know no pretense that I have to the honour Lord Gray is pleased to do me; but if His Lordship chooses to own me it certainly is not my business to deny it." His father, Philip Gray, son of a successful merchant, was born in 1676, and, towards his thirtieth year, he married Miss Dorothy Antrobus, a Buckinghamshire lady, who, with her sister Mary, kept a Milliner's Shop in the City. In spite of their shop, however, these ladies belonged to a genteel family. Their remaining sister, Anna, was the wife of a prosperous country lawyer—Mr. Jonathan Rogers—and the two brothers, Robert and Thomas Antrobus, were fellows at Cambridge colleges and afterwards were tutors at Eton. These two sisters, Mary and Anna, Anna's husband—Mr. Rogers, and the two brothers must be mentioned in detail because they were of great importance in Gray's life.

托马斯·格雷的生平极其简单。他于1716年12月26日出生在伦敦康希尔区其父的家中。说来也奇，他的身世鲜为人知。晚年，在其声名鹊起之时，福法尔郡（英国苏格兰原郡名）的格雷男爵声称与他有血缘关系。格雷只说了这样一句："我无意炫耀格雷阁下乐于赐予的荣耀，但如果

# III

阁下选择赐之于我,那我无权予以拒绝。"他的父亲菲利普·格雷1676年生于一个富商之家,年近而立之年与白金汉郡的多乐茜·安卓布斯结了婚。当时多乐茜与妹妹玛丽在城里经营一家女帽商店。尽管如此,她们两姐妹都出生于有教养的家庭。她们还有一位妹妹叫安娜,嫁给了一位富有的乡村律师——乔纳森·罗杰斯先生。她们的两个兄弟,罗伯特和托马斯·安卓布斯则是剑桥学院的校友,后来成了伊顿公学的导师。在这里要详细说一下玛丽和安娜两姐妹、安娜的丈夫——乔纳森·罗杰斯先生和他们的两兄弟,是因为他们对格雷的一生有着极其重要的意义。

\*

Thomas was one of twelve children, and the only one who grew to manhood. He was, apparently, neglected by his father and was brought up by his Mother and Aunt Mary. Their home life at Cornhill was rendered miserable by the father's cruelties and the boy's Uncle, Robert Antrobus, took him to live at his own house at Burnham, Buckinghamshire. There is a picture of the young Gray, aged fifteen, in the Fitzwilliam Museum at Cambridge. He has a broad brow, very sharp nose and chin, large eyes and a rather pert expression.

托马斯家里共有12个兄弟姐妹,但唯有他一人长大成人。显然,他的父亲对他疏于教养,是母亲和姨母玛丽将他拉扯长大。由于父亲的残暴,他们在康希尔的家中过得非常悲惨。他的叔叔,罗伯特·安卓布斯把他接到了自己家里——白金汉郡的伯纳姆生活。在剑桥大学的菲茨威廉博物馆,挂着一张年仅15岁的小格雷的画像。画中的他有着宽阔的额头,高挺的鼻梁,尖尖的下巴和一双大眼睛,颇有些傲慢无礼的神情。

\*

At Eton he made some important friendships—Horace Walpole, Richard West, George Montague. Afterwards Gray went up to Cambridge, where Walpole followed him later. We see at this time the hardships his Mother had been enduring, for a Law Case was discovered in which the poet's Mother states that for the whole of her married life she had received no support from her husband.

在伊顿公学，他结交了几位重要的朋友——霍拉斯·沃波尔、理查德·韦斯特和乔治·蒙泰格。后来，格雷前往剑桥，不久沃波尔也尾随而至。在一个对外公开的法律案件中，格雷的母亲宣称在她的婚后生活中，没有从丈夫那里得到任何资助。由此，我们可以看出他母亲在这段时间里所经历的艰难生活。

IV

\*

I, personally, regard these unfortunate family circumstances as affecting more importantly the whole of Gray's after-life than any other thing. He was probably of the masculine-feminine temperament from birth—a temperament much more clearly understood to-day than it was then, but these circumstances of his father's brutality and his Mother's self-sacrificing love, must, undoubtedly, have encouraged his reserved pride, his shrinking from the rudeness and impertinence of strangers, his apprehension of life, his fear of intimacies.

我个人认为，这样不幸的家庭环境对格雷的整个后半生的影响远甚于其他任何事情。很可能从一出生，他就具有阳刚和娇柔的双重性格。父亲的无情和母亲无私的爱，这些影响无疑助长了他的冷漠高傲，他逃避粗暴对陌生人无礼，他对生活的理解以及对亲密的恐惧也受此影响。这种性情在今天比在当时更能被人理解。

\*

For the rest, the main crises of his history were four: first, his foreign tour with Horace Walpole, secondly, the shelter and friendship he found at Pembroke College, thirdly, the publication of his poems, and fourthly, his friendship with Bonestetten at the very close of his life.

此外，格雷的人生主要经历了四个关键阶段：第一，与霍拉斯·沃波尔的国外游学经历；第二，在彭布罗克学院找到的庇护与友谊；第三，诗集的出版；第四，晚年与波内斯特腾结下的友谊。

\*

It may be that the only really happy months he was ever to know were those of the first part of his tour with Walpole. It was Horace

# V

Walpole's proposition that they should start together on a Grand Tour. My great-great-great-great Uncle has been criticised so often for coldness of heart and selfishness of disposition, that it is pleasant to know that, with regard to this Tour, Walpole was altogether generous and kind. He was to pay all Gray's expenses but Gray was to be absolutely independent. Also, without letting Gray know, Walpole made out his Will before starting and so arranged that had he died while abroad Gray would have been his sole legatee.

也许在他的回忆里，唯一真正快乐的时光是与沃波尔游学的最初几个月。当初是霍拉斯·沃波尔建议他们应该一起进行这样一次游学。上溯四代，我的曾叔父因铁石心肠、性情自私，常常遭人批评，令人欣慰的是，对于这次游学，沃波尔是如此的慷慨善良。他打算为格雷支付所有的费用，但格雷想完全自理。此外在格雷不知情的情况下，沃波尔在出发前写下了遗书。遗书上说，如果他在这次国外旅行中客死他乡，格雷将是他遗产的唯一受赠人。

\*

So abroad on their famous Tour they went and I like this little picture of Gray in Paris, a real young fop if ever there was one: "He complains that the French Tailor has covered him with silk and fringe and has widened his figure with buckram, a yard on either side. His waistcoat and breeches are so tight that he can scarcely breathe; he ties a vast solitaire around his neck, wears ruffles at his fingers' ends, and sticks his two arms into a muff." Gray, in fact, was absolutely delighted with his new existence. He writes to West: "I could entertain myself this month merely with the common streets and the people in them." But, of course, in addition to the "common people" he and Walpole lived in the highest society and did all the most elegant things.

于是他们开始了这次著名的游学。我喜欢格雷在巴黎的这张小画像，那确实是一个典型的花花公子形象："他抱怨法国的裁缝给他裹上绸缎，缀上流苏，在他的身形两侧用硬麻布各加宽一码。他的背心和马裤紧得让他几乎无法呼吸；脖子上挂着一粒巨大的宝石，指末戴着褶饰，两只手臂牢牢地插在了手筒里。"事实上,格雷对这种新生活感到欣喜若狂。他写信给韦斯特说:"这个月只要在大街上逛逛,在人群中走走,我就能让自己很开心。"当然,他与沃波尔不仅仅是"普通人",他们过的是上流社会的生活,做的是高贵风雅的事儿。

\*

Later in the Tour, alas, there was a quarrel, and the two friends separated. They were to be apart for three years.

在随后的旅程中,这两位好朋友发生了争执,以致分道扬镳,一别便是3年。

\*

With the close of this Tour the rest of Gray's outside story is simple.

游学生活结束以后,格雷其他的外出经历随之简单了。

\*

His father died in 1741. He 1ived for a while with his Mother at Stoke Poges and, in 1742, proceeded to Peterhouse College at Cambridge, taking his Bachelor's Degree in Civil Law and was installed as a resident of that College. From then until 1759 he divided his life between Cambridge and Stoke Poges and, although he was a member of Peter-house, it was at Pembroke College that he found his real friends and made his true life.

格雷的父亲于1741年过世。随后他回到斯多克·波吉斯与母亲住了一段时间。1742年,他进入剑桥大学彼得豪斯学院继续深造,获得民法学士学位后,定居在学院里。从那时起直至1759年,他一直在剑桥和斯多克·波吉斯两地来回奔波。虽然身为彼得豪斯学院的一名教员,但正是在彭布罗克学院他才遇到了真正的朋友,真正的人生随之开始。

\*

The rest of his public story is to be found in his poetry and his letters: of the real inner man we know, even to-day, far too little.

其他众所周知的故事在他的诗歌和书信中都可以一览无余,不过,直到今天,我们对这位诗人的真实内心世界仍知之甚少。

# VII

\*

It was in the Summer of 1757 that Horace Walpole set up a Printing Press at Strawberry Hill. Gray's Pindaric Odes were the first publications from this Press. Two thousand copies of the Odes were rolled off and it is interesting to note that Gray received forty guineas for this publication and that this was the only money he ever gained by literature. With this publication Gray arrived in a moment of time at the head of the living English Poets. Thomson was dead, Collins hopelessly mad, Johnson no longer writing poetry, Goldsmith and Cowper still unheard of. It was, in a way, a fortunate time for his reputation and yet the whole sum of Gray's poetry is small indeed in quantity, although almost always perfect in quality.

1757年夏天，霍拉斯·沃波尔在草莓山创办了一家出版社。格雷的"品达体颂歌"是这个出版社最早发行的出版物。颂歌共发行了2000余册，有意思的是，这次出版让格雷赚了40畿尼的金币，而这是他唯一一次通过出版文学作品而获得的收益。这部作品使格雷一度成为当时英语诗人中的领军人物：汤姆森已经死去；柯林斯变得疯疯癫癫，无可救药；约翰逊已不再写诗；戈登·史密斯和考珀还是无名小卒。从某种程度上来说，这个时期是格雷成名的黄金时期，虽然大部分作品质量上乘，但是数量确实少之又少。

\*

My business here is with the Elegy, and I do not propose any general discussion of Gray's poetry, but it is interesting to consider as to how his reputation has endured and his fame withstood the impertinent criticism of time. Two things did, for a hundred years at least, much to damage Gray's reputation. First, Johnson's attack in *The Lives of the Poets* and, secondly, the stupid boorishness of Mason's *Life*. Johnson's criticism is, of course, on the side of common sense. He was no friend of the whimsical and would toss his great head and rumble his body round at anything that seemed to him fustian or melodrama. But he is on weak ground when he criticises qualities in Gray's poetry derived from Greek influences. The whole temper of Greek literature was foreign to Johnson. I can imagine, too, that Johnson was out of sympathy with the womanly side of Gray's nature. He, more than most men, was impatient of effeminacy. Of course, against Johnson's denials there were the enthusiastic affirmations of men like Gibbon and Hume, but then came the Lake School again, who considered that Gray had been grossly over-praised. Time has, however, its own fashion of dealing with reputations and we may say that Gray is as firmly fixed in the high places of English Letters as any writer of whom we can think. It is quite certain now that no change of taste or period in the future can shake the Elegy from its throne. Why is that? Why is it that a poem rather platitudinous in idea and exceedingly domestic in detail should be one of the dozen classics of English Poetry? First, let us see how the poem came into being: Gray's Aunt, Miss Mary Antrobus, died suddenly at the age of sixty-six at Stoke Poges on the 5th November, 1749. Gray felt this loss very greatly and wrote a most tender and beautiful letter to his Mother on the subject. The death of his Aunt seems to have brought to his memory "The Elegy In a Country Church-Yard", begun seven years before. Tradition tells that he took it up again at Cambridge in the Winter of 1749, and finished, as he had begun it, at Stoke Poges. The last touches were added on the 12th June, 1750. On that same day he wrote to Horace Walpole: "Having put an end to a thing whose beginning you have seen long ago I immediately send it to you. You will, I hope, look upon it in the light of a thing with an end to it: a minute that most of my writings have wanted and are likely to want." Walpole at once perceived the greatness and endurance of this poem. Nevertheless its appearance in the world was of a most casual and careless nature. Walpole's enthusiasm caused him to hand the poem about from friend to friend and he even distributed manuscript copies of it without Gray's permission. When, in 1751, a periodical coolly informed Gray that it was printing his "ingenious poem", Gray wrote to Walpole in no pleasant humour, and insisted that Dodsley

IX should print it immediately from Walpole's copy but without Gray's name. Five days after this letter, on the 16th February, 1751, Dodsley published a large quarto pamphlet, anonymous, priced sixpence, entitled *An Elegy Wrote In a Country Church-Yard*. It was preceded by a short preface unsigned but written by Horace Walpole. Further than this we need not pursue the many editions of the famous poem. Its bibliography is a most complicated affair.

在这里我所要讨论的是《墓畔挽歌》这部作品，且我不打算就格雷的诗歌做任何一般性的讨论，但探讨一下他的名声为何经久不衰，经得起一代代人中肯的批评，确是件趣事。至少在一百年的时间里有两件事情，对格雷的名声造成了负面影响。第一，约翰逊在《诗人生活》中对格雷的抨击；第二，梅森在《生活》中的无知与庸俗。约翰逊的批评当然是根据常理来的。他并非怪异之人，对于他所认为的空洞或离奇之事，他都嗤之以鼻，并无休止地争论下去。但他批判格雷的诗歌风格受希腊文学影响时，理由并不充分。约翰逊并不了解希腊文学的整体特征。我也可以猜想，约翰逊对格雷女人般的天性是嗤之以鼻的。他比大多数男人更无法容忍这种柔弱。当然，约翰逊对格雷的否认遭到了诸如吉本和休谟等人的反对，他们对格雷表示热情洋溢的肯定。但后来湖畔派诗人又认为人们对格雷的评价过高。然而，时间自有其对声誉的评判标准。可以说，格雷的崇高地位像任何一位我们耳熟能详的作家一样，已在英国文学中深深扎根。如今，我们可以肯定，不管人们的欣赏水平如何改变，或是岁月如何变迁，都无法动摇这首《墓畔挽歌》至高无上的地位。这是为什么呢？为什么一个在主题上如同老生常谈，在细节处理上又极为普通的诗歌可以成为英语诗坛的经典作品之一呢？首先，让我们来了解一下这首诗歌是怎样被创作出来的。1749年11月5日，格雷的姨母、66岁的玛丽·安卓布斯小姐猝死于斯多克·波吉斯。格雷感到非常伤心，所以他以此为主题，给他母亲写了一封最伤感、最优美的信。姨母的死，使他想起了他7年前开始写的《墓园挽歌》。据说在1749年的冬季，他在剑桥再次提笔续写，正如这首诗歌始于斯多克·波吉斯，同样在这里结束。1750年6月12日，他又对诗歌做了最后的润饰。在同一天，他写信给霍拉斯·沃波尔说道："这份稿件你在很久以前就看到我着手了，我一完成马上就给你寄过去。我希望，你会把它当成一个有结局的故事：这个结局是我以往大多数作品所缺少的，也将是以后作品缺少的。"沃波尔立刻意识到这首诗歌将是伟大的传世之作。不过谁都不会想到，这首诗歌的诞生却是如此的不经意。沃波尔满怀热情地把这首诗歌传给一个个朋友欣赏，甚至未经格雷的允许就把手稿的复件进行分发。1751年，某期刊轻描淡写地转告格雷称其已在印刷这首"天赋异曲"，对此，格雷以讽刺的口吻致信沃波尔，要求多兹利出版社根据沃波尔的复稿立刻出版这首诗歌，但绝不能用格雷的名字。5天后，即1751年2月16日，多兹利出版社便把这首诗以匿名形式印刷成四开本大的小册子出版了，书名为《墓畔挽歌》，每册定价6便士。霍拉斯·沃波尔为该书写了简短的序，但并未署名。此外，我们无需赘述这部名著的其他很多版本。关于它的参考文献已是最复杂的了。

\*

Edmund Gosse has written that the Elegy "retained a higher reputation in literature than any other English poem, perhaps than any other poem in the World written between Milton and Wordsworth. The fame of 'The Elegy' spread to all countries, and has exercised an influence on all the countries of Europe, from Denmark to Italy, from France to Russia. With the exception of certain works of Byron and Shakespeare, no English poem has been so widely admired abroad." Gosse wrote these words fifty years ago, but they are more true than ever to-day, and we may well ask ourselves with a kind of astonishment as to where lie the seeds of immortality in this gentle and quiet poem. The answer lies, I think, first in the fact that the Elegy possesses that double interest which must accompany any artistic work of universal fame, namely, that its application is both general and particular. Its theme is the imminence to every human soul alive of the mystery of Death and the deep truth that this conclusion to all human endeavour has no regard for place or power, fame or obscurity. There is very little Christian comfort in the spirit of the poem. There is no dogmatic teaching, only a sadness that is too true to be resented. The theme and direction of the poem are universal. The detail is so particular that it catches and holds an isolated and rare beauty.

艾德蒙·戈斯写道，这首挽歌"在文学史上的地位超过了任何一首英文诗歌，也许都超过了在弥尔顿(1884—1940)和华兹华斯(1770—1850)诗歌时代的任何一首诗作。这首《墓畔挽歌》享誉海内外,对欧洲所有国家——从丹麦到意大利,从法国到俄罗斯——都产生了影响。除了拜伦和莎士比亚的某些作品外,还没有哪一首英文诗在国外受到过如此广泛的赞誉"。这些话是戈斯在五十年前写的,但今天看来更为令人信服。我们也许会惊讶地问自己,这样一首温柔恬静的诗歌,它那不朽的闪光点究竟是在哪儿呢?我觉得,答案首先在于《墓畔挽歌》拥有世界知名艺术作品必备的双重价值,也就是说,该作品既适用于一般,又适用于个别。它所表达的主题揭示了神秘的死亡向每个存在的人类灵魂的逼近,并阐述了这样一个真谛,即:所有人类的努力都无关乎地位或权力,无关乎声名显赫或默默无闻。在诗歌精髓中,鲜少提及基督的宗教关怀,也没有过多的说教,有的只是过于真实而无法表达愤懑的悲哀。诗歌的主题和方向都具有普遍性。细节处理是如此独特,以至它捕捉住了一种脱俗而又罕有的美。

\*

In literature the regional has always a chance of immortality, for if the author can make the reader feel that there is in this square of ground that he is describing a beauty unique and eternal, his writing will be kept alive as a guiding hand to that beauty. We feel about such writers as Turgenieff, Tchehov, Maupassant, Thoreau, that their great appeal lies in their catching mysteriously the very tang and substance of their own native soils. *Boule-de-Suif* holds in its few pages the very essence of France: a Tchehov short story gives us two or three lonely figures moving across the snow or waiting for a train at a little side station and we are in Russia. In the same way it is the supreme merit of Gray's Elegy that it captures and holds for ever a certain England unique in the world's history. This England is simple enough in its detail. The thin Church Spire piercing a smoky blue, the long fields like lawns running down to a lazily broken stream spreading its way through tall grasses; the village street, the ploughman driving his horses against the skyline, the cawing of the rooks in the elms, the little graveyard with its fading memories, the shouts of boys at play, thinned and softened by the country air. These are the things with which Gray deals. You may say that it has been done often enough in English before, this quiet English scene. Yes, all the way from Chaucer to Edmund Blunden. Gray has done it better than any other. Why? Because, I think, his almost desperately fastidious mind was allied triumphantly to an eagle sharpness of vision. Every word in the Elegy is rung again and again as a coin upon a plate to be tested, and the exact vision has the shining, lovely perfection of jewels and refined gold.

在文学中，有地域特色的事物很有可能得以不朽，因为如果作者能够让读者在他所描述的疆域里感到一种独特而永恒的美，那么他的作品就会成为指引人们通向美的指针，从而经久不衰。我们觉得这样的作者，如屠格涅夫、契诃夫、莫泊桑、梭罗等，他们的巨大吸引力在于他们传神地抓住了本国的特性和实质。《羊脂球》用几页的文字就抓住了法国的精髓；契诃夫的一篇短篇小说，描述了两三个孤独的人物，或在雪中穿行，或在小小的边台上等候火车，此时我们在俄国。同样，格雷《墓畔挽歌》的精妙在于他捕捉到了在世界历史上英格兰的某种独特之美。此时的英格兰在其细节之处分外简单：教堂的尖顶直刺灰蓝的天空，广袤的田野像一片巨大的草坪，蔓延至一条缓缓流动的溪流；溪水一路蜿蜒，穿过高高的草丛；在天空的映衬下，耕夫赶着马走在乡村的街道上；榆树上白嘴鸦在呱呱叫着，小墓园和它褪色的记忆，男孩嬉戏时的喊叫声，这些都在乡村的空气中变得稀疏、柔和、淡却。这就是格雷在诗中所描写的景物。你可能会说在这之前的英文诗歌中都有涉及这种宁静的英国场景。我想是的，从乔叟到艾德蒙·布伦顿，一直有诗人描写这样的场景。但格雷描写得比任何人都要好。这是为什么呢？我认为，是由于他把极度挑剔的思想与鹰一般敏锐的洞察力成功地结合在了一起。《墓畔挽歌》中的每个字都像一枚落入碟中的硬币，不断发出回响，接受着考验，准确的洞察力闪烁着珠宝和纯金般动人完美的光芒。

※

## XIII

And finally, when all is said, one returns to the true and touching simplicity of Gray's picture, and the sad mournful music of one who feels that a sort of courageous resignation is the only true philosophy.

HUGH WALPOLE

最后,当你回归到格雷的真实而感人的朴素画面和那忧伤缅怀的音乐中,你会体会到,唯一真实的人生哲学是一种无畏的顺其自然。

休·沃波尔

# 文稿注解

# A NOTE UPON THE TEXT

*It is known that Gray wrote the Elegy between 1746 and 1750. Three manuscript drafts are in existence. One manuscript, now at Eton College, is probably the original draft; and the text of this manuscript is printed in the last pages of the present edition. Although the first printing was issued anonymously in 1751, an edition issued in 1768 received the poet's final approbation. Therefore the text used in the present edition to accompany Miss Parker's engravings follows closely the approved edition of 1768.*

众所周知,格雷的挽歌创作于1746年到1750年间,现存共有三份手稿。如今存放在伊顿学院的一份很可能是最初的手稿,此手稿的文本印在现行版本的最后几页。挽歌曾于1751年匿名首发,但1768年的再版获得了诗人的最终许可。因此在现行版本中,配有帕克小姐版画的版本与1768年的获准版最为接近。

#  THOMAS GRAY'S ELEGY

# 挽歌

托马斯·格雷 著

文爱艺 译

晚霞，敲击了
　　离别的丧钟，
低哞的牛群
　　在草地上悠然回响，
归家的农夫
　　拖着疲惫的脚步离去，
这世界剩下的
　　唯有黄昏伴我的幽冥。

*The Curfew tolls*
　　*the knell of parting day,*
*The lowing herd*
　　*winds slowly o'er the lea,*
*The plowman homeward*
　　*plods his weary way,*
*And leaves the world*
　　*to darkness and to me.*

苍茫的景色
  正渐渐地从眼前逝去,
萦绕着的空气
  弥漫着肃穆的寂静,
只有嗡嗡的甲虫
  在空中飞舞环绕,
沉沉的钟声
  催眠着远处的羊群:

Now fades the glimmering
  landscape on the sight,
And all the air
  a solemn stillness holds,
Save where the beetle
  wheels his droning flight,
And drowsy tinklings
  lull the distant folds;

只听见远处
　　常春藤爬满的塔楼里
阴郁的猫头鹰
　　似在对月亮诉怨
漫游之人无端闯入
　　她的私密之境，
惊扰了这片古老
　　独栖领地的幽静。

Save that from yonder **3**
　　ivy-mantled tow'r
The moping owl
　　does to the moon complain
Of such, as wand'ring
　　near her secret bow'r,
Molest her ancient
　　solitary reign.

峥嵘的老榆树下,
　　浓密的紫杉树荫底,
剥落的草皮
　　鼓起零乱的荒堆,
每一个灵魂
　　归宿在他那狭小的墓穴中,
乡野淳朴的先人
　　在此长眠。

*Beneath those rugged elms,*
　　*that yew-tree's shade,*
*Where heaves the turf in*
　　*many a mould'ring heap,*
*Each in his narrow*
　　*cell forever laid,*
*The rude forefathers*
　　*of the hamlet sleep.*

微风轻唤起
　　芬芳的清晨，
稻草棚下的燕子
　　在低声地呢喃，
雄鸡尖锐的啼鸣，
　　像号角的回响，
却再也不能将那些先辈
　　从浅梦中唤醒。

The breezy call
　　of incense-breathing Morn,
The swallow twittering
　　from the straw-built shed,
The cock's shrill clarion,
　　or the echoing horn,
No more shall rouse them
　　from their lowly bed.

壁炉中的烈焰，将不再

　　为他们添暖，

忙碌的主妇，也不再

　　为他们做晚饭；

孩子们不再跑来跑去

　　咿呀相告父亲的归来，

也不再爬上父亲的双膝

　　争享那令人羡慕的亲吻。

*For them no more the*

　　*blazing hearth shall burn,*

*Or busy housewife*

　　*ply her evening care;*

*No children run*

　　*to lisp their sire's return,*

*Or climb his knees*

　　*the envied kiss to share.*

辛勤的镰刀
　　带来满意的收获，
坚硬的土地
　　他们犁出沟壑；
赶着牲畜下地
　　生活如此惬意！
他们猛力挥刀
　　林木不禁折腰！

Oft did the harvest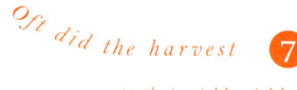
　　to their sickle yield,
Their furrow oft the
　　stubborn glebe has broke;
How jocund did they drive
　　their team afield!
How bow'd the woods
　　beneath their sturdy stroke!

莫让野心

　　鄙夷他们的辛苦，

嘲弄他们朴实的快乐，

　　以及卑微的运道；

也不要让显贵

　　带着讥讽的嘲笑，

去聆听穷苦人

　　短暂而简朴的人生。

*Let not Ambition*

　　*mock their useful toil,*

*Their homely joys,*

　　*and destiny obscure;*

*Nor Grandeur hear*

　　*with a disdainful smile,*

*The short and simple*

　　*annals of the poor.*

炫耀的门第，
　　显赫的权势，
以及所有美
　　和财富所给予的一切，
都同样等候在那
　　必然的时刻：
荣耀之路
　　无不归于黑暗的墓穴。

**9**

*The boast of heraldry,*
　　*the pomp of pow'r,*
*And all that beauty,*
　　*all that wealth e'er gave,*
*Awaits alike*
　　*th' inevitable hour:*
*The paths of glory*
　　*lead but to the grave.*

骄傲的人,

 切莫把这些归咎于过失,

如果怀念

 未能为其竖起丰碑,

那么请在那漫长的过道

 和雕有回纹饰的拱顶

充溢洪亮的颂歌

 扬起赞美的曲调。

   impute to These the fault,
If Mem'ry o'er their Tomb
   no Trophies raise,
Where thro' the long-drawn
   and fretted vault
The pealing anthem
   swells the note of praise.

饰画的瓮碑

　　栩栩的半身像

难道能使

　　逝者复活？

荣耀之声

　　难道能使死灰复燃？

谄媚之音

　　也能俘获死神冷漠的耳根？

*Can storied urn* **11**

　　*or animated bust*

　　　*Back to its mansion*

　　　　*call the fleeting breath?*

　　*Can Honour's voice*

　　　*provoke the silent dust,*

　　*Or Flatt'ry soothe*

　　　*the dull cold ear of Death?*

荒冢遗忘之地
　　沉睡的亡灵
或许曾孕育过
　　天才的火种灵焰的心；
手，本可以
　　将权柄掌握，
或将令人心醉
　　神迷的竖琴出神入化地弹奏。

*Perhaps in this* **12**
　　*neglected spot is laid*
　　*Some heart once pregnant*
　　　　*with celestial fire;*
　　*Hands that the rod of empire*
　　　　*might have sway'd,*
　　*Or wak'd to extasy*
　　　　*the living lyre.*

他们眼中的智慧女神
　　　永不会翻开
她那
　　　时光隐忍的史册；
贫寒尘封了
　　　他们高贵的襟怀，
凄苦冻结了灵魂深处
　　　奔涌的泉流。

But Knowledge to their eyes
　　　her ample page
Rich with the spoils of time
　　　did ne'er unroll;
Chill Penury repress'd
　　　their noble rage,
And froze the genial
　　　current of the soul.

世上多少璀璨的珠宝
　　纵使光芒夺目也无人察觉，
用尽一生探究
　　最终遗落在幽暗的海底洞窟；
世间多少的花儿
　　注定吐艳后无人怜赏，
虚耗的芳香
　　在荒芜的空气中消散。

Full many a gem ⑭
　　of purest ray serene,
The dark unfathom'd
　　caves of ocean bear:
Full many a flower
　　is born to blush unseen,
And waste its sweetness
　　on the desert air.

那个叫汉普登的村民,
　　英勇无畏
反抗当地的
　　乡绅恶霸；
缄默不语无名的弥尔顿
　　在此安息,
那个叫克伦威尔的人
　　豪情无愧于民族的血气。

*Some village Hampden,*
　　*that with dauntless breast*
*The little Tyrant*
　　*of his fields withstood;*
*Some mute inglorious*
　　*Milton here may rest,*
*Some Cromwell guiltless*
　　*of his country's blood.*

要博得满场
 元老们的掌声,
就要轻视痛苦的威胁
 抛却生死,
要在这片乐土上
 撒播富饶,
就要以民族之眼
 研读自己的历史,

Th' applause of list'ning
 senates to command,
The threats of pain
 and ruin to despise,
To scatter plenty
 o'er a smiling land,
And read their hist'ry
 in a nation's eyes,

他们受命运裁决：

 行为受到约束
不单成长的德行受限，

 恶行也遭抑止；
禁绝从杀戮中

 夺取王权，
却对人类关上

 慈悲为怀的大门，

Their lot forbad:

 nor circumscrib'd alone
Their growing virtues,

 but their crimes confin'd;
Forbad to wade through

 slaughter to a throne,
And shut the gates

 of mercy on mankind,

掩埋真相的
    苦痛挣扎，
平息愧疚的
    瞬时赧颜，
抑或堆积起
    骄奢的神龛
点燃那香炉中
    缪斯的神焰。

*The struggling pangs* **18**
    *of conscious truth to hide,*
*To quench the blushes*
    *of ingenuous shame,*
*Or heap the shrine*
    *of Luxury and Pride*
*With incense kindled*
    *at the Muse's flame.*

远离喧嚣纷纭
　　人世间的明争暗斗，
他们审慎的理想
　　从未尝试过改变；
沿着凄冷幽静的
　　命运之谷
他们不声不响地
　　迈着从容的脚步。

*Far from the madding* **19**
　　*crowd's ignoble strife,*
*Their sober wishes*
　　*never learn'd to stray;*
*Along the cool*
　　*sequester'd vale of life*
*They kept the noiseless*
　　*tenor of their way.*

纵然这些尸骨
　　免受沧桑的凌辱
残破的碑铭
　　依旧挨近竖立，
还有拙劣的韵语
　　凌乱的刻划，
恳请过往的路人啊
　　进献一声哀婉。

Yet ev'n these bones
　　from insult to protect
Some frail memorial
　　still erected nigh,
With uncouth rhimes and
　　shapeless sculpture deck'd,
Implores the passing
　　tribute of a sigh.

无名的诗神，拼出了
  他们的名号与生辰，
在那名望之乡
  添上碑铭：
她又在周围
  刻上数篇圣典经文，
引导乡野的卫道士
  怎样去归黄土。

*Their name, their years, spelt* **21**
  *by th' unletter'd muse,*
*The place of fame*
  *and elegy supply:*
*And many a holy text*
  *around she strews,*
*That teach the rustic*
  *moralist to die.*

有谁愿意成为
　　无名之辈，
坦然撇下
　　这忧喜交织的此生，
离开这充溢欢乐的
　　温暖之地，
而不再留恋
　　驻足顾盼回望？

For who to dumb 22
　　Forgetfulness a prey,
This pleasing anxious
　　being e'er resign'd,
Left the warm precincts
　　of the cheerful day,
Nor cast one longing
　　ling'ring look behind?

逝去的灵魂

　　依偎在柔情的胸膛，

紧闭的双眼

　　尽洒虔诚的眼泪；

即使在坟墓里

　　大自然也在哭泣，

即使我们化为灰烬

　　也依然跳动着隽永的火花。

On some fond breast **23**

　　the parting soul relies,

Some pious drops

　　the closing eye requires;

Ev'n from the tomb

　　the voice of Nature cries,

Ev'n in our Ashes

　　live their wonted Fires.

你想起了
　　那些默默无闻的死者，
用这些诗句
　　叙述他们无奇的一生；
若神眷顾
　　由沉思独自指引，
某位志趣相投之人
　　将来叩问他们的命运，

For thee who, mindful 24
　　of th' unhonour'd Dead,
Dost in these lines
　　their artless tale relate;
If chance, by lonely
　　contemplation led,
Some kindred Spirit
　　shall inquire thy fate,

白发的乡下人
　　或许会说：
"我们常常在清晨
　　看见他
脚步匆忙
　　被露水打湿衣衫
登上高坡的草地
　　看朝阳升起。

*Haply some hoary-headed*
　　*Swain may say,*
'*Oft have we seen him*
　　*at the peep of dawn*
'*Brushing with hasty steps*
　　*the dews away*
'*To meet the sun*
　　*upon the upland lawn.*

"在远方那棵低垂的
　　山毛榉树下
苍老的古木藤根
　　层层屈蟠，
他常中午时分
　　将慵懒的身躯舒展，
一边凝视着
　　泉边的涓涓溪水。

There at the foot 26
　　of yonder nodding beech
'That wreathes its old
　　fantastic roots so high,
'His listless length at
　　noontide would he stretch,
And pore upon
　　the brook that babbles by.

"在那树林边上,
　　他正带着嘲弄的微笑,
喃喃说着
　　他天马行空般的漫想,
时而垂头丧气,悲苦欲殇,
　　就像一曲惆怅,
疯狂失意地,
　　沉浸在无望的爱里。

"Hard by yon wood,
　　now smiling as in scorn,
Mutt'ring his wayward
　　fancies he would rove,
Now drooping, woeful wan,
　　like one forlorn,
Or craz'd with care,
　　or cross'd in hopeless love.

"一天清晨，在他惯去的山上
　　我没有像往常那样看见他，
也许他刚穿过石楠丛
　　或来到他最喜爱的树旁；
第二天，
　　不论我寻踪溪畔，
还是踏遍草坪，搜遍树林，
　　却都不见他的踪影；

*'One morn I miss'd him*
　　*on the custom'd hill,*
*Along the heath*
　　*and near his fav'rite tree;*
*Another came;*
　　*nor yet beside the rill,*
*'Nor up the lawn,*
　　*nor at the wood was he;*

"翌日突然哀乐声声
　　悲伤唱着挽歌
载着他慢慢步向墓园
　　我们见他隐现。
且请前来一读
　　（因你是识字的）那些
镌刻在丛老荆棘下
　　石头上的碑铭："

*'The next with dirges* **29**
*　　due in sad array*
*Slow thro' the church-way*
*　　path we saw him borne.*
*Approach and read*
*　　(for thou can'st read) the lay,*
*Grav'd on the stone*
*　　beneath yon aged thorn:"*

# THE EPITAPH

墓志铭

"他的躯体在这里安息

    躺在这大地的膝上,

运气与名望

    从未垂青与他。

聪明的学识

    从未介怀他卑微的出身,

却是忧郁

    为他打上了终身的烙印。

*Here rests his head* **30**

    *upon the lap of Earth,*

*A Youth to Fortune*

    *and to Fame unknown.*

*Fair Science frown'd not*

    *on his humble birth,*

*And Melancholy*

    *mark'd him for her own.*

"他慷慨大方,

　　灵魂虔诚,

上天也同样,以慷慨

　　回报他:

他把拥有的一切

　　全都献给了悲伤,哪怕是一滴泪珠,

而在天堂之地,他获得了(他所

　　期望的)挚友。

*Large was his bounty,*

　　*and his soul sincere,*

*Heav'n did a recompense*

　　*as largely send:*

*He gave to Mis'ry*

　　*all he had, a tear,*

*He gain'd from Heav'n ('twas*

　　*all he wish'd) a friend.*

31

"无需深入追寻
　　逐一展露他的美德，
或从可怕的地方
　　将他的弱点一一翻现，
（在那里，他们
　　颤抖的渴望得到安宁，）
那里是天父与上帝
　　坦荡的胸怀。"

*No farther seek* **32**

*his merits to disclose,*
*Or draw his frailties*
　　*from their dread abode,*
*(There they alike*
　　*in trembling hope repose,)*
*The bosom of his Father*
　　*and his God.*

# THE TEXT
# OF THE FIRST EDITION

*Printed from the original MS. now preserved in the Memorial Buildings of Eton College.*

第一版文稿

该版原始印稿现存于伊顿公学的纪念馆中

The Curfeu tolls the Knell of parting Day,
The lowing Herd wind slowly o'er the Lea,
The Plowman homeward plods his weary Way,
And leaves the World to Darkness & to me.

Now fades the glimm'ring Landscape on the Sight,
And now the Air a solemn stillness holds;
Save, where the beetle wheels his droning flight,
Or drowsy Tinklings lull the distant Folds.

Save that from yonder ivy-mantled Tower
The mopeing Owl does to the Moon complain
Of such as wandring[1] near her secret Bower
Molest her[2] ancient solitary Reign.

\*

(1) *stray too is written above wandring.*
(2) *& pry into is written above Molest her.*

长夜将至,敲响了白昼离别的丧钟,
牛群低哞,在青草地上悠然迂回,
疲惫的农夫,步履沉重,缓缓归家,
把世界留给了黑暗与我。

微光中的景色,从眼际消逝而去,
空气里弥漫着肃穆的寂静;
只有甲虫嗡嗡地盘旋飞行,
昏沉的铃声,催眠着远处的羊群。

只听见那披裹着常青藤的塔楼里
阴郁的猫头鹰对着月亮诉苦
怨人无端闯入它的私密之地
打扰了这片古老而僻静的领地。

Beneath those rugged Elms, that Yewtree's shade,
Where heaves the turf in many a mould'ring heap,
Each in his narrow Cell for ever laid
The rude Forefathers of the Hamlet[3] sleep.

Forever sleep the breezy Call of Morn,
Or swallow twitt'ring from the strawbuilt shed,
Or chaunticleer so shrill or ecchoing horn,
No more shall rouse them from their lowly bed.

For them no more the blazeing hearth shall burn,
Or busy huswife ply her evening care;
No children run to lisp their sire's return,
Nor climb his Knees the coming[4] Kiss to share.

Oft did the Harvest to their Sickle yield;
Their Furrow oft the stubborn Glebe has broke;
How jocund did they drive their Team a-field!
How bow'd the Woods beneath their sturdy Stroke!

Let not Ambition mock their useful[5] Toil,
Their rustic Joys & Destiny obscure:
Nor Grandeur hear with a disdainful Smile
The short & simple Annals of the Poor.

\*

(3) *Village has been struck out and Hamlet written above.*
(4) *envied is written above and doubtful is written in margin.*
(5) *homely is substituted for useful in margin.*

峥嵘的老榆树下，浓密的紫杉树荫里，
草皮上鼓起了许多凌乱的荒堆，
每一个灵魂，长眠在他那狭小的墓穴中
小村庄里，朴实的先人在此安息。

清晨的微风轻轻召唤睡着的人们，
燕子在稻草棚下呢喃，
雄鸡尖声打鸣，回声犹如号角，
却再也不能唤醒，沉睡在低矮石床上的先人。

熊熊的炉火，不再为他们燃烧，
忙碌的主妇，不再会赶她们的夜活；
孩子们不再会呀呀地报告父亲的到来，
更别提攀父双膝，分享那期待的轻吻。

辛勤的收割，总为他们带来满意的收获；
坚硬的土地常常被犁出沟壑；
他们多么欢欣地赶着牲口下地！
他们猛地一砍，连大树都弯腰鞠躬！

不要让雄心嘲笑他们有用的劳作，
他们纯朴的快乐，默默无闻的命运：
高贵，也切莫带着鄙夷的微笑
去聆听穷苦人家，短暂而平凡的一生。

The Boast of Heraldry the Pomp of Power,
And all, that Beauty, all that Wealth, e'er gave
Awaits alike th' inevitable Hour.
The Paths of Glory lead but to the Grave.

Forgive, ye Proud, th' involuntary Fault,
If Memory to these no Trophies raise,
Where thro' the long-drawn Ile, & fre tted Vault
The pealing Anthem swells the Note of Praise.

Can storied Urn, or animated Bust,
Back to its Mansion call the fleeting Breath?
Can Honour's voice awake[6] the silent dust,
Or Flattery sooth the dull cold Ear of Death?

1. Perhaps in this neglected Spot is laid
   Some Heart, once pregnant with celestial Fire,
   Hands, that the Reins of Empire might have sway'd,
   Or waked to Ecstasy the living Lyre:

7. Some Village Cato [7] with dauntless Breast
   The little Tyrant of his Fields withstood;
   Some mute inglorious Tully here may rest;
   Some Caesar, guiltless of his Country's Blood.

\*

(6) *provoke is substituted for awake in margin.*
(7) *A word is lost through the fraying of the paper at a crease.*

门第的吹嘘，权势的炫耀，
所有美和财富，所给予的一切
却都是为了静候，那不可避免的时刻。
荣耀之路，无不通往黑暗的墓穴。

骄傲人，原谅这些人的无心之失，
如果回忆，未能为其竖起丰碑，
那么请让那漫长的过道，雕花的拱顶
充溢洪亮的颂歌，扬起赞美的曲调。

铭刻事略的瓮碑，栩栩的半身像，
能否唤回，那已逝去的灵魂？
难道荣誉的声音能唤醒沉寂的死灰，
谄媚，怕也难打动死神冷漠的耳根。

1.在此荒芜之地，兴许埋藏着
　　某颗曾充满烈焰的心灵，
　　一双手，本可以挥舞那帝王的权杖，
　　也可以拨起让人心醉神迷的竖琴：

7.某个英勇无畏的村民加图□
　　够胆反抗地头蛇的豪强贵戚；
　　某个默默无闻的唤作塔利的人，或许安息此处；
　　那个叫恺撒的人，豪情无愧于民族的血气。

But Knowledge to their eyes her ample Page,
Rich with the Spoils of Time, did ne'er unroll;
Chill Penury had damp'd[8] their noble Rage,
And froze the genial Current of the Soul.

Full many a Gem of purest Ray serene,
The dark unfathom'd Caves of Ocean bear.
Full many a Flower is born to blush unseen,
And wast its Sweetness on the desert Air.

Th' Applause of listening Senates to command,
The Threats of Pain & Ruin to despise,
To scatter Plenty o'er a smiling Land
And read their Hist'ry in a Nation's Eyes,

Their Fate[9] forbad: nor circumscribed alone
Their struggling[10] Virtues, but their Crimes confined;
Forbad to wade thro' Slaughter to a Throne,
And shut the Gates of Mercy on Mankind

The struggleing Pangs of conscious Truth to hide,
To quench the Blushes of ingenuous Shame
And at[11] the Shrine of Luxury & Pride
With[12] Incense hallowd in[13] the Muse's Flame.

\*

(8) *depress'd repress'd written above.*
(9) *Lot written above.*
(10) *growing written above.*
(11) *Crown written above at.*
(12) *Burn is struck out and With inserted above.*
(13) *kindled at written below, by instead of in written above.*

但是知识从不在它们眼前展开,
它历代累积而琳琅满目的书卷;
贫寒削减了他们高贵的襟怀,
冻结了他们灵魂里涌出的暖流。

世间多少晶莹剔透的珍珠
深埋在幽暗而不可测的海底。
世间多少花儿吐艳而无人怜赏
虚耗的芳香飘散在荒凉的空气中。

要赢得在场所有议员的掌声,
就要蔑视痛苦,淡忘生死,
在欢乐的大地上撒播富饶
设身处地,研读他们的历史,

他们受宿命裁决:行为受到约束
不单挣扎的善行阻绝,恶行也遭抑止;
正如禁绝杀戮,而获得王权,
却对人类关上,慈悲为怀的大门

掩埋真相的痛苦,
平息了愧疚带来的瞬时赧颜
在奢侈与骄傲的神龛上
缪斯的火焰中焚香被神圣化。

The thoughtless World to Majesty may bow
Exalt the brave, & idolize Success
But more to Innocence their Safety owe
Than Power & Genius e'er conspired to bless

And thou, who mindful of the unhonour'd Dead
Dost in these Notes their artless Tale relate
By Night & lonely Contemplation led
To linger in the gloomy Walks of Fate

Hark how the sacred Calm, that broods around
Bids ev'ry fierce tumultuous Passion cease
In still small Accents whisp'ring from the Ground
A grateful Earnest of eternal Peace

No more with Reason & thyself at Strife;
Give anxious Cares & endless Wishes room,
But thro' the cool sequester'd Vale of Life
Pursue the silent Tenour of thy[14] Doom.

Far from the madding Crowd's ignoble Strife,
Their sober Wishes never knew to stray:
Along the cool sequester'd Vale of Life
They kept the silent[15] Tenour of their Way.

\*

(14) *In thy the y is struck out and eir written above.*
(15) *noiseless written above.*

无主的世界向威严行礼致意
颂扬英勇之人,膜拜成功
但他们的安全归功于无知
而非权力和天赋的共同赐福

虽你想起了那些,默默无闻的死者
用这些诗句,叙述他们朴实的故事
伴随着暗夜与独自沉思的指引
在灰蒙的宿命之途徘徊

听,神圣的平静无处不在
呵斥每一个焦躁的心灵停止喧嚣
虽只是地底传来的只声片语
却都满怀着永享安宁的热忱

不要再让自己和理智作斗争;
给焦虑关怀和无尽的渴求留一点空间,
穿越那条凉爽僻静的人生溪谷
继续你命定的那份孤寂旅程。

远离了喧嚣人群的明争暗斗,
他们审慎的理想从未学着偏离:
沿着清新幽静的命运之谷
他们始终走在寂静的人生之路。

Yet even these Bones from Insult to protect
Some frail Memorial still erected nigh
With[16] uncouth Rhime, & shapeless Sculpture deckt
Implores the passing Tribute of a Sigh.

Their Name, their Years, spelt by th' unletter'd Muse
The Place of Fame, & Epitaph supply
And many a holy Text around she strews,
That teach the rustic Moralist to die.

For who to dumb Forgetfulness, a Prey,
This pleasing anxious Being e'er resign'd;
Left the warm Preccints of the chearful Day,
Nor cast one longing lingring Look behind?

On some fond Breast the parting Soul relies,
Some pious Drops the closing Eye requires:
Even from the Tomb the Voice of Nature cries,
And buried Ashes glow with Social Fires.

For Thee, who mindful &c: as above.

If chance that e'er some pensive Spirit more,
By sympathetic Musings here delay'd,
With vain, tho' kind, Enquiry[17] shall explore
Thy once-loved Haunt, this long-deserted Shade.

\*

(16) *With substituted for another word, perhaps In, which has been inked out.*
(17) *Mitford reads inquiries.*

纵然这些尸骨，免受岁月的侮辱
残破的碑铭，依旧在周遭竖立
□还有粗制的韵诗，和走样的雕饰
恳请过路人进献一声哀息。

不识字的缪斯拼出了他们的名字，他们的年龄
也添上了碑铭，在那名望之乡
在她的周边，刻上数篇圣典经文，
引导乡村的卫道士，归于黄土。

谁甘愿被遗忘，不闻一言，
永远放弃这忧喜；
离开温暖的快乐时光，
不再留恋地驻足回望？

那逝去的灵魂依偎在充满温情的胸膛，
紧闭的双眸，落下虔诚的泪珠；
即使在坟墓里大自然也在哭泣，
埋葬的灰烬闪烁着尘世的火焰。

你想起了：同上。

如果还有更多哀思的灵魂，
被这儿深为同情的沉思所耽搁，
徒劳却友好地打听到
你那曾经深爱过的幽魂，早已被遗弃在孤独的角落。

Haply some hoary headed Swain shall say,
Oft have we seen him at the Peep of Dawn
With hasty Footsteps brush the Dews away
On the high Brow of yonder hanging Lawn

Him have we seen the Green-wood Side along
While o'er the Heath we hied, our Labours done,
Oft as the Woodlark piped her farewell Song
With whistful Eyes pursue the setting Sun.

Oft at the Foot of yonder hoary[18] Beech
That wreathes its old fantastic Roots so high
His listless Length at Noontide would he stretch,
And pore upon the Brook that babbles by.

With Gestures quaint now smiling as in Scorn,
Mutt'ring his fond Conceits[19] would he[20] rove,
Now drooping, woeful wan,[21] as one forlorn,
Or crazed with Care, or cross'd in hopeless Love.

One Morn we miss'd him on th'customd[22] Hill,
By[23] the Heath[24] and at[25] his fav'rite Tree.

\*

(18) *spreading is written above, nodding in the margin.*
(19) *wayward fancies is written above.*
(20) *wont to is struck out, loved is written above and struck out, finally would he is written above.*
(21) *The line originally stood Now woeful wan, he droop'd. drooping is inserted above and he droop'd is struck out.*
(22) *ac⌈customed⌉ ac struck out.*
(23) *Along written above.*
(24) *side is written after Heath and struck out.*
(25) *Near written above at.*

一位白发的乡下人或许向你倾诉，
我们常常在黎明时刻看到他
步履匆忙将露水也带走
攀上远处高耸崖顶的草地

当我们看到他穿过绿林斜坡
结束劳作的我们，便会急速奔过那石楠丛堆，
像森林中云雀般，吹奏着告别的歌曲
用留恋的眼神追逐着夕阳西下。

在那棵灰白的山毛榉下
悠长而奇特的树根直缠绕至高处
在正午时分，伸展出他那倦怠的躯干，
凝视着小溪潺潺流过身旁。

古怪的手势伴着嘲讽般的微笑，
喃喃说着他所编织的奇思幻想，
时而垂头丧气，悲苦欲病，似无依凄凉，
又或忧心忡忡，或失意情场。

某一天清晨，在他惯去的山上，我没碰到他，
或穿过石南丛或来到他最喜爱的树林。

Another came, nor yet beside the Rill,
Nor up the Lawn, nor at[26] the Wood was he.


[27]The next with Dirges meet in sad Array
Slow thro[28] the Church-way Path we saw him born
Approach & read, for thou can'st read the Lay
Wrote[29] on the Stone beneath that[30] ancient Thorn:


There scatter'd oft the earliest of ye Year[31]
By hands unseen are frequent[32] Vi lets found
The Robin[33] loves to build & warble there
And little Footsteps lightly print the Ground.


Here[34] rests his Head upon the Lap of Earth
A Youth to Fortune & to Fame unknown
Fair Science frown'd not on his humble birth
And Melancholy mark'd him for her own


Large was his Bounty & his Heart sincere;
Heaven did a Recompence as largely send.
He gave to Mis'ry all he had, a Tear.
He gained from Heav'n; twas all he wish'd, a Friend


\*


(26) *By written above.*
(27) *Written and struck out There scatter'd oft, the earliest.*
(28) *By written above.*
(29) *Graved carved written above.*
(30) *yon written above.*
(31) *Spring struck out and year written above.*
(32) *showers of written above. Vi lets MS. In a later draft Gray wrote vi'lets.*
    *Probably he hesitated whether to use here the apostrophe or the full word.*
(33) *Redbreast written above.*
(34) *The Epitaph is written along the outer margin.*

第二天早晨，不论我寻踪溪畔，
还是踏遍草坪，甚或搜遍树林，却还不见他的踪影。

第三日，偶遇送丧的行列，带着悲伤，吟唱挽歌
载他缓缓向墓园而去
走近去念念，因为你是识字的吧
那首写在那丛老荆棘下石头上的诗句：

在远古时期，总有那看不见的双手
四处撒播着，随处可见的紫罗兰
知更鸟喜爱在那里筑巢缠绵
小小的脚轻轻地在地面上落下脚印。

他的头颅躺在了这里，躺在这大地的膝上
这个年轻人不名一文、默默无闻
善智之神毫不介怀，他的卑微出身
忧郁则在他身上打上烙印

他慷慨大方，为人诚恳；
上天也同样，以慷慨作为回报。
他的一切都献给了悲伤，哪怕是一滴泪珠。
天堂之地，他获得了所望的挚友

No further seek his Merits to disclose,
Nor seek⁽³⁵⁾ to draw them from their dread Abode
(His frailties there in trembling Hope repose)
The Bosom of his Father & his God.

\*

(35) *think is written above seek.*

无需深入追寻,逐一展露他的美德,
也不要试图从可怕的地方将他的弱点一一挖出
(在那里,他的弱点哆嗦着希望得到休歇)
那里是天父与上帝的坦荡胸怀。

# 跋

文爱艺

**ELEGY WRITTEN IN A COUNTRY CHURCH-YARD** 是我10年前在塞纳河边的书摊上淘得的；雨后的巴黎，令书格外清新，我一眼就看中了这本不厚的宝贝，那散发着神秘气息的美在艾格尼斯·米勒·帕克木刻插图中荡漾。

在很长的时间，它是我的枕边书，陪我走遍了整个欧州。

我把它译为《墓畔挽歌》；这是一部思想之书，它的深刻正好同它的厚薄成反比，它的魅力恰巧与我们窘迫的现实契合！

此诗最初是为了哀悼他的好友里查德·韦斯特，内容却远远超越了对具体人物的哀思；诗通过对乡村墓地的描写，表达了对生活在社会底层人民的深切同情；由于贫困，农民不能发挥自己的才能，但他们身上没有"骄""奢"，虽然"贫瘠"，但有"德性"和"天良"，他们就是自然本身。诗赞扬了他们纯朴善良的品质，为他们没有机会施展天赋和才华而惋惜，同时也表现了对权贵骄奢糜烂生活的谴责、人间虚荣的嘲讽和蔑视。

诗充分体现了民主思想，表述了人生亘古不变的规律和结局：无论你来自哪里，贫穷还是富有，美丽还是丑陋，强大还是柔弱，最终归于黄土。权势，名望……在强大的命运面前，都显渺小。

作者表达的不是绝望的悲鸣，不是黯然的哀伤，而是对人生的忧思。

诗并不复杂，它简单、自然、纯洁得如一幅画那样展现在你的面前，你在为它所溢出的境界而陶醉的同时，不禁被它显现的优美气息折服。

全诗以质朴的情感，细腻的笔触，出尘的口吻，把命运二字娓娓道来，读罢，人生的真相扑面而来。

《墓畔挽歌》凝结的民主思想，是解决我们纷乱现实的钥匙，因为它所张扬的精神，正是我们现在所缺乏的，它所彰显的情感，恰恰是我们目前所缺失的！

《墓畔挽歌》凝聚了人类的社会情绪，并且以完美的形式表达了这种情绪。它突破了诗歌本身所具有的文学艺术价值，而具有很高的社会价值。它清晰地表达了超越人生所应达到的境界。

《墓畔挽歌》用自然的语言揭示了命运残酷的现实：人生除了死亡没有第二个结局。它表达了人生的哲理：功名利禄，不过是过眼云烟。

《墓畔挽歌》在文学史上的地位超过了任何一首英文诗，它恬静的气息，闪烁着太阳般温暖动人的光芒。

文爱艺

2012年4月5日草于清明雨水中／2017年9月6日修订于日本东京

本书特装版,全球限量发行3003册,按印制顺序编号,排序从1至3003止。

您手中的此书,编号为:

中央编译出版社

**本书荣获2012年中国最美的书**

图书在版编目(CIP)数据

墓畔挽歌 /（英）托马斯·格雷著；文爱艺译.—
北京：中央编译出版社，2017.12

ISBN 978-7-5117-3376-4

Ⅰ.①墓… Ⅱ.①托… ②文… Ⅲ.①叙事诗－
英国－近代 Ⅳ.①I561.24

中国版本图书馆CIP数据核字(2017)第190745号

## 墓畔挽歌

| | |
|---|---|
| 出 版 人： | 葛海彦 |
| 出版统筹： | 贾宇琰 |
| 责任编辑： | 邓永标 |
| 执行编辑： | 舒　心 |
| 书籍设计： | 赵　清 |
| 责任印制： | 刘　慧 |
| 出版发行： | 中央编译出版社 |
| 地　　址： | 北京西城区车公庄大街乙5号鸿儒大厦B座(100044) |
| 电　　话： | (010)52612345(总编室)　　(010)52612365(编辑室) |
| | (010)52612316(发行部)　　(010)52612346(馆配部) |
| 传　　真： | (010)66515838 |
| 经　　销： | 全国新华书店 |
| 印　　刷： | 北京环球画中画印刷有限公司 |
| 开　　本： | 950毫米×1194毫米　1/32 |
| 字　　数： | 40千字 |
| 印　　张： | 4.5 |
| 版　　次： | 2018年1月第1版 |
| 印　　次： | 2018年1月第1次印刷 |
| 定　　价： | 68.00元 |
| 网　　址： | www.cctphome.com　　邮　　箱：cctp@cctphome.com |
| 新浪微博： | @中央编译出版社　　微　　信：中央编译出版社(ID：cctphome) |
| 淘宝店铺： | 中央编译出版社直销店(http://shop108367160.taobao.com)　(010)55626985 |

本社常年法律顾问：北京市吴栾赵阎律师事务所律师　闫军　梁勤
凡有印装质量问题，本社负责调换。电话：(010)55626985

## 延伸阅读

### 《小王子》

首次推出打动全球亿万读者的超级畅销精品《小王子》；完美译本，原创插图，还原《小王子》经典阅读，老幼皆宜的文本本色。本书入围2017年中国最美图书。

### 《文爱艺诗集》

本书在浩如烟海的出版物中脱颖而出，在畅销20多年后，2011年又被评为"中国最美的书"；2012年被评为"世界最美的书"，畅销不衰。